MAC'S SPORTS REPORT

CONCUSSION COMEBACK

Book design by Jake Nordby
Illustrations by Simon Rumble

Published in the United States by Jolly Fish Press, an imprint of North Star Editions, Inc.

First Edition
First Printing, 2018

This is a work of fiction. Names, characters, places, and incidents are either the product of the author's imagination or are used fictitiously, and any resemblance to actual persons living or dead, business establishments, events, or locales is entirely coincidental.

Library of Congress Cataloging-in-Publication Data (pending)
978-1-63163-228-0 (paperback)
978-1-63163-227-3 (hardcover)

Jolly Fish Press
North Star Editions, Inc.
2297 Waters Drive
Mendota Heights, MN 55120
www.jollyfishpress.com

Printed in the United States of America

MAC'S SPORTS REPORT

CONCUSSION COMEBACK

BY KYLE JACKSON
ILLUSTRATED BY SIMON RUMBLE

PREDATORS SHOW GRIT ON THE GRIDIRON

by Mac McKenzie

The game wasn't pretty. Constant drizzle softened the field. Players' cleats ground away at the turf. Halfway through the first quarter, the field had been churned to mud. Featuring two of the top-scoring teams in the state, this was supposed to be a high-scoring affair. Coyote Canyon Middle (now 3–0) had been averaging a solid 25 points a game; East River (2–1) was coming off a 46–8 blowout victory. But the weather made it almost impossible to move the chains. It often appeared difficult for players to merely stay on their feet.

The Predators made the adjustment first. Usually they feature a balanced offense—half pass, half run. But their strategy quickly became all-run, all the time. At first they had some success. Running back Carter Sanchez charged his way to several first downs. At the end of the first quarter, he slipped (literally) into the end zone.

That ended up being the game's only points.

All told, quarterback Ryan Mitchell attempted

just six passes, and only one of them in the second half.

With 1:08 remaining in the fourth quarter, the Predators got called for a holding penalty that pinned them to their own one-yard line. It was third and 16, so a first down seemed unthinkable. Mitchell was going to hand the ball off to Sanchez and hope he could gain a few yards and give the Predators' punter some room to kick.

Mitchell took the snap, faked to throw, then reached out to hand off the ball to Sanchez. An opposing lineman drilled Mitchell to the field while Sanchez broke through the line of defense and raced toward the first-down marker before slipping and landing on the wet turf too.

Still, Sanchez had barely crossed the line for the first down. That was enough to knock the Raiders off their game.

A few plays later, the final whistle blew. The Predators had held off the Raiders for another win.

"It wasn't pretty," Ryan Mitchell said after the game, "but we found a way to win."

CHAPTER 1

Stewart "Mac" McKenzie, eighth grade sports reporter, wakes up worried.

Not a lot, but a little.

He's slightly concerned because of what happened at the game last night—or, anyway, what *might* have happened.

Late in the game, after the Predators got called for a holding penalty, after the Predators huddled up again, and after Ryan took another snap and handed it to running back Carter Sanchez, a player for East River tackled Ryan to the ground.

Mac isn't sure whether it was a dirty play.

Ryan had just attempted a deep pass, so maybe the East River player thought Ryan had the ball and was going to throw again. If that's what happened, then the tackle made sense.

Or maybe the East River player was frustrated about losing the game and took his frustration out on a defense-less quarterback. If *that's* what happened, then it was a total cheap shot.

But that's not what makes Mac a little worried.

At this point, it doesn't really matter why the East River player tackled Ryan. All that matters is that he *did* tackle him . . . hard.

It was a truly crushing blow.

Which also isn't what worries Mac.

Crushing blows are just a part of football, after all.

What worries Mac—not much, but a little—is that he thinks he saw Ryan's neck snap back and his head smash against the field.

Mac was sitting on the sidelines when it happened. He had to convince his parents that sitting on the sidelines was necessary for his work; they worried that he and his wheelchair were too close to the action. But he liked to watch the game from there because he could feel its violence and intensity. As a reporter, he liked to have a sense of what it was like to actually be on the field or court when playing a sport.

Sometimes, though, that meant he didn't have the best view of the game.

Especially in football.

Big bodies often stood in the way of the action.

Last night's rain didn't help either.

But despite having his view blocked, and despite all

the rain and the mud, Mac's fairly sure he saw Ryan's head slam into the turf. A couple of linemen quickly turned and noticed Ryan on the ground and helped him to his feet.

That's when Mac saw something else that slightly worried him: Ryan took one wobbly step and then fell to the ground again.

Granted, it was muddy and very slippery. That's why Mac isn't too concerned. The problem is that it didn't look to Mac like Ryan slipped; it looked like he collapsed.

The linemen helped Ryan to his feet again as the game clock ticked to zero.

All the Predator players standing on the sideline rushed onto the field to celebrate the victory.

Mac backed up to the track and waited.

A few minutes later, as the players and coaches left the field, Mac was able to find Ryan Mitchell.

"Can I ask you a few questions, Ryan?"

Ryan stepped to his left and leaned against the fence separating the track from the bleachers. A few of his Predator teammates punched his shoulder pads as they hustled to the locker room.

"Congrats on the big win," Mac said.

"Thanks." Ryan had taken his helmet off. The helmet

had molded his flat top so it looked like he had a button on top of his hair.

"Can you tell me what was going on in your head when you made that last play of the game?" Mac asked. "Was it your decision or Coach's to pass the ball instead of run it?"

Ryan didn't answer at first. He squinted . . . because of the rain, maybe? Or because he was trying to come up with an answer?

Finally, he said, "It wasn't pretty, but we found a way to win. Look, I've gotta go."

It was this comment that worried Mac the most. After all, it didn't answer Mac's question—not even close. In fact, it was just a general and relatively meaningless statement. Good enough for Mac to use in his article, but he couldn't help but wonder: If Ryan *had* slammed his head on the field, and if he *had* fallen instead of slipped, then was it possible that he was having trouble thinking straight? Was it even possible that he had forgotten the biggest play of the game?

Probably not. Ryan's vague answer could be explained in other ways. Mac had made the mistake of asking two questions, back to back, without giving Ryan a chance to answer the first. Besides, athletes talked in clichés all the time. Then again, Mac had always found Ryan's answers to questions to be really thoughtful. Maybe he had so much adrenaline going after the win that he couldn't be as thoughtful as he usually was?

Maybe.

But what if there was another reason? A head-injury reason?

When Mac gets to school, he decides, he'll ask Ryan some follow-up questions.

CHAPTER 2

As usual, Mac gets to school early. Way too early to follow up with Ryan about last night's game and interview.

The reason he likes to get to school so early isn't for his journalism. It's to play basketball.

His district team's captain's practices begin in a week or so. For now, he practices on his own in the gym.

"Hey, Mac."

Okay, he's not technically, totally alone. Diego Lunez, a backup guard for the school team, is usually there too.

"Hey," Mac tells him.

But beyond saying hi to each other, they don't say much else. It's not that they don't like each other—they do. In fact, Mac has a deep respect for Diego's work ethic, and he's pretty sure the feeling is mutual.

Day after day, they both arrive at school early to shoot hundreds of shots before any of the other kids have set foot in the school.

Diego shoots on one end of the court; Mac shoots on the other.

The only sounds are made by their basketballs:

bouncing on the hardwood court, clanking off the rim, or swishing through the net.

Mostly swishing through the net.

Especially on Mac's end of the court. If there's one thing that Stuart McKenzie does better than write, it's shoot.

One time Mac's dad, before dropping Mac off, said, "It must be a good time to get some thinking done."

Mac had no idea what he meant. He still doesn't.

The reason Mac loves shooting isn't to think about things. It's to *not* think about things.

When he's shooting, the only things he's aware of are the rim and the basketball, leaving his hand and spinning backward as it arcs and then splashes through the net.

The only thing he thinks about is how many shots he's made in a row.

At some point he swivels around and sees that Diego must have finished his own shooting routine because he's nowhere to be found.

Mac hustles across the court, hoping he didn't zone out the first period bell.

It isn't difficult to track Ryan down. After all, they're in band together.

Today, there's a sub, which should make it even easier to talk to Ryan.

Mac plays trombone; Ryan plays percussion. And because they're in different sections, they don't sit next to one another.

But whenever there's a sub, some students swap instruments. A saxophone player might switch with a flute player. A trumpet player spends the class period playing the triangle or the xylophone. The students do the swapping secretly. It's a prank, after all. And they somehow always manage to get away with it.

Mac has never taken part in the prank. For one thing, he's not so sure they actually *do* get away with it. It sounds so awful in the band room that it's hard to believe the sub doesn't realize what's going on. More than likely, the sub just doesn't think it's worth calling the class out.

In any case, it's not that Mac's scared of getting into trouble; he just doesn't want to give up his spot. Right now he's first chair, which means he's considered by Mr. Paulsen, the band director, to be the best trombone player in the school. First-chair players get to play the solos at band concerts.

Truthfully, Mac doesn't care very much about these solos or even about being good at the trombone. He thinks a lot more about the next game than he does the next concert. If he had to list his priorities, they would start with writing about sports and end with playing them, or vice versa.

But he's still not about to let Dave Corcoran take his first chair, especially not three weeks before their fall concert.

Dave is second chair, and unlike Mac, he cares *a lot* about being considered the best trombone player. Which would be fine, if the kid wasn't such a jerk about it. His constant critiquing of Mac's playing is bad enough. "Your rhythm was off," he'll say to Mac. Or, "You were flat." Dave sometimes literally tries to sabotage him. One of the things about playing trombone is that there are lots of times when you're not expected to actually play. Your job at those times is to carefully count out the measures until you're supposed to join the song. This counting can get boring, so during practice, trombone players trade off who has to do it. Sometimes, when it's Dave's turn to do the counting, he lifts his trombone to his mouth and puffs his cheeks at the wrong time. The first time he did this, Mac mimicked Dave . . . and played a loud note when it was just supposed to be the flutes playing. He looked over at Dave and saw that he'd lowered his trombone and continued "innocently" counting.

What really gets to Mac is the way Dave goes behind his back. The other day, Mr. Paulsen came up to Mac and said, "I hear you haven't been practicing very much. I just want to make sure everything's okay. I need you to be ready for your solo in 'Battle Hymn of the Republic'." Mac assured him that he must have heard wrong; Mac's been practicing plenty. He didn't need to ask Mr. Paulsen where he'd gotten this false information.

It's actually kind of ironic. Mac might have quit band a long time ago and given up his spot to Dave if Dave wasn't, well, Dave. Mac's primary motivation for staying in band isn't making great music; it's refusing to let evil win.

(Well, that and dessert. After every concert, his parents take him to Baker's Batch, the local coffee and pie shop, and let him have the two best foods in the world: a chocolate malt, no whipped cream, and a slice of strawberry pie with real strawberries and none of that canned syrup nonsense.)

Today, for the first time, Mac decides to give up his first chair, even if it means Dave will get to claim it for the day.

Paul Yilek, a percussionist like Ryan Mitchell, agrees to trade with Mac.

Of course, his plan could always backfire on him. *What if Ryan decides to swap instruments too?*

Mac doubts this will happen. He's spoken enough with Ryan to know the kid is a rule-follower, especially in the middle of the season. He wears a suit and tie on every game day, even though it's not required. Mac asked him about it once, and he said, "I want everyone to know that I'm committed to leading our team to victory." Mac wasn't entirely sure what the connection was between a suit and either leadership or victory, but he was still impressed.

As everyone warms up before the first song at today's practice, Ryan shuffles up to the snare drum. Mac is about ten feet away, sitting next to the cymbals, which he's chosen intentionally. It doesn't seem like many songs require the cymbals, and when they do, it's only for a few noisy clangs. The less he has to play, he figures, the less likely he'll mess up the song—and the more time he'll have to watch Ryan and come up with questions to ask him.

Mac is about to ask one of these questions when the sub waves her arms to get everyone's attention.

She announces her name—Ms. Becker—picks up the

conducting wand from the podium in front of her, and waves it to start the first song.

They're supposed to be playing a compilation of movie theme songs: *Jaws*, *Jurassic Park*, *Indiana Jones*, *Star Wars*.

But it's difficult to determine when one song ends and another begins. Trumpets blare. Flutes murmur. Saxophones squeal.

For a while, it becomes oddly quiet. That's because a bunch of students aren't really playing. They're faking it, pressing buttons on their new instruments at random, puffing their cheeks without actually blowing. Mac looks across the room and sees that, sure enough, Dave Corcoran is sitting in Mac's spot. Paul Yilek is next to him, pushing and pulling the slide of Mac's trombone back and forth for no apparent reason.

SCREECH!

Mac's pretty sure the sound comes from a misfired saxophone. It's fairly loud, but nothing out of the ordinary for days with a sub.

What *is* out of the ordinary is Ryan's reaction. It's dramatic enough to catch Mac's attention out of the corner of his eye. Ryan drops his drumsticks and covers his ears. He tilts his head, shuts one eye, and squints the other.

Mac asks him, "Are you okay?"

The blaring of the instruments drowns out his question, so he wheels over to Ryan and taps him on the shoulder.

Ryan's face is now in the crook of his arm. He lifts his head and his eyelids and sees Mac. He must not have noticed Mac before, because his eyes instantly open in surprise. His knees are bent (and wobbly?), but he stands straight up.

"Are you okay?" Mac asks again.

"Fine," Ryan says, paging through the songbook to find his place. It's only then that he realizes he doesn't have his drumsticks. He bends his legs again, gets in a crouch, reaches for the sticks.

BANG!

It's another bad note, and it sends Ryan's hands back to his ears.

"Are you sure?" Mac asks.

Still with one arm over his face, Ryan reaches, blindly, for the drumsticks.

That's when the lights start blinking on and off. Mac turns to the front of the room. Ms. Becker is flicking the light switch, trying to get everyone's attention. She probably got sick of waving her conductor's wand fruitlessly.

Mac turns back to Ryan in time to watch him stumble and stagger out of the room.

CHAPTER 3

Mac does the same thing he always does.

He follows the story.

This time, following the story means literally following Ryan.

Mac swivels his chair and, after asking for a hall pass from the sub, races after Ryan. Mac enters the hall in time to see Ryan turn the corner, down another hallway. Ryan's not staggering anymore; with every step he's picking up speed.

So is Mac.

Mac calls out, "Wait up!" But he isn't sure whether Ryan hears him.

What exactly is he running from? The noise? The band room? Me?

There's only one way to find out.

He whips around another corner in time to see Ryan lunge into a bathroom halfway down the hall.

The bathroom door swings shut, but a few seconds later, Mac is there to open it again.

At first, it appears to be empty. Then he sees the sneakers under the stall door.

"Ryan?" Mac says.

The sneakers lift up, disappear.

"Ryan," Mac says again. "I know you're in here. I saw your shoes."

Pause.

"Fine," Ryan says through the door. "You caught me."

He must use his foot to kick the door, because it swings open. Mac has to wheel back to avoid getting hit.

Ryan's in there, sitting on top of a lidded toilet, his legs raised.

"Caught you? I was just hoping to ask some questions." Before launching into the important questions, he has to ask, "What are you doing?"

Ryan looks at his raised legs, lowers them, shrugs. "Hiding. It worked in a movie I saw."

"Hiding from . . . ?"

"You."

"Me?" Mac asks.

"Your questions."

"So you know what I'm going to ask."

Ryan shrugs again. "You want to know if I have a concussion."

"Do you?"

"On the record, absolutely not. I feel totally fine."

"Off the record?" Mac asks.

"I think you already know the answer to that question," Ryan says.

"Well then, what are you going to do?"

"What do you mean, what am I going to do? I'm going to keep playing—just like everyone used to until concussions became such a big deal."

Mac can't believe what he's hearing. Or seeing. Just a few minutes ago, Ryan literally fell to the floor because of a misplayed note and he's currently rubbing his temples as he talks. But his plan is to pretend he's okay?

"Concussions didn't just become a big deal," Mac says. "They've always been a big deal. We just didn't know it."

Ryan shrugs, still kneading his temples.

"You get that concussions are a big deal, right?" Mac asks.

"What I get is that our next game is against Forrest View, and we can't afford to lose it."

"Ryan, this is crazy. You've got to tell Coach Jorgenson what happened."

"No, I don't. And you don't either. You *can't*. This whole conversation was off the record."

He stands up and leaves, blinking extra hard—the way people blink when they have a splitting headache.

Mac doesn't know what to do. He goes through the day wrestling with his options.

He knows what he *wants* to do: Head straight for Coach Jorgenson's office and tell him, "Your quarterback suffered a concussion last night and shouldn't be allowed anywhere near the field."

That would definitely be the safest thing. Thanks to his bruised brain, Ryan's clearly not thinking straight.

But Mac also knows he can't do that—not without breaking journalistic ethics.

Then again, do journalistic ethics really exist when you're a middle school reporter writing for a middle school paper?

Some people might not think so, but he's not one of them. To him, he might as well be writing for *Sports Illustrated* or *ESPN*. He's never understood athletes who tell themselves, "It's just a game," or "This isn't the pros." Why would you take your own life less seriously than you take other people's lives? Mac wasn't a middle school reporter; he was a reporter who happened to also go to middle school.

That meant that when someone went off the record, Mac wouldn't—he couldn't—publish what they said.

Could he?

What if doing so would prevent serious physical harm? What if he didn't publish Ryan's words, but simply told the coach in private?

Were there times when breaking the rules was the right thing to do?

If you're racing to the hospital, isn't it okay to drive over the speed limit and run a few lights?

Was this situation the same as that?

Mac didn't know.

What he *did* know was that he was running out of time. The day's last class had ended a few minutes ago; soon, football practice would start. When it did, Ryan's bruised brain was probably going to get bruised some more.

No, Mac didn't know what to do. But he knew he had to do something.

That's why he finds himself racing through the halls. He swerves through the cafeteria and then takes a sharp left down the hallway next to the gymnasium. From there he takes a right and hurtles down another hall. He punches the automatic door button, but gets to the door before it's completely open. He rams through it anyway.

He cuts through the parking lot, and makes a beeline for the football field.

Somehow or other, he needs to get Ryan out of practice before the tackling starts.

Mac finally arrives at the field and realizes, to his relief, that he's wrong.

He doesn't need to stop practice. He doesn't need to stop players from slamming their pads into one another.

The players aren't *wearing* any pads. They're scattered along the field in shorts and shirts.

Mac should have known there wouldn't be any pads in sight. After all, it's the day after a game, and Coach Jorgenson *always* makes these days noncontact, walk-through practices. That means there won't be any tackling.

Sure, it's still stupid for Ryan to be out there when he should probably be sleeping and recovering, but Mac doesn't think that's worth breaking his journalistic code over.

He sits there awhile, catching his breath.

"No interviews during practice, McKenzie."

Mac turns. Coach Jorgenson is standing next to him, a whistle sticking out of the side of his mouth. Mac's never understood how Coach can talk so clearly without removing the whistle.

"Don't you have other sports you should be covering right now? Sports that are currently playing games or matches?" Coach Jorgenson asks.

Mac knows Coach Jorgenson well enough to also know he's not really hounding him. Coach does have a rule against interviewing his players on practice days, but

he also trusts Mac to follow it. Unlike a lot of coaches, Coach Jorgenson doesn't treat reporters like the enemy. It was actually his idea to have Mac sit on the sidelines with the team during games.

"Still," Coach says around his whistle, "if you want to ask my players why they're not wearing long sleeves on the first cold day of the year, I'll allow it."

Mac looks back at the field. Sure enough, the players are in T-shirts.

"It's not that cold," Mac says.

It's not like he can see the players' breaths or anything. Mac is wearing a hoodie and jeans, and that's plenty warm enough.

"It will be. Wait a month, and they'll *still* try to play without sleeves. It happens every year. I'm thinking of making a rule: no sleeves, no play."

Mac's surprised by how animated Coach is right now. It takes a lot to rile him up. Even more surprising, the whistle has fallen from his mouth.

"Why haven't you?" Mac asks.

"Why haven't I what?"

"Made a rule."

"I keep thinking common sense will prevail. Or science.

Science already has a rule: No sleeves, you might get frost-bite. Why do I have to come up with another rule?"

You have to give Coach credit: He's practicing what he preaches. Unlike the players, he's bundled up pretty good. Underneath the flat-brimmed baseball hat he always wears is a stocking cap. It's not just his head that is layered. He also has a turtleneck shirt beneath his sweatshirt.

"It's part of the culture," Mac says, even though he realizes he's telling Coach something he already knows. "Football players don't wear sleeves because it proves they're tough."

It's true. It'll be the middle of winter and below-zero temperatures, and even then, a lot of NFL players won't wear sleeves.

"That's an observation," Coach says, "but it's not an argument."

Mac waits for him to explain what he means.

"Sure, football culture encourages players to play with bare arms. But that doesn't mean it's a good idea. If it's not a good idea, then football should change its culture."

"Easy as that?" Mac asks.

"Why not?" Coach says. "If something is stupid, stop doing it."

Mac takes a pen out of his pocket and kiddingly

pretends to write on his hand. "Just to be clear—are you saying football culture or your players are stupid?"

Coach laughs. "Yeah, probably should have told you this is off the record."

"Everything's off the record these days," Mac says.

"What do you mean?"

"Nothing." Mac is trying to sound casual, but he feels suddenly flustered. He can't believe he hinted at his off-the-record conversation with Ryan Mitchell. "I better go."

Coach squints at him, clearly curious. But then he says, "Don't let me keep you, McKenzie."

As Coach opens the fence door and moves toward the field, he blows the whistle that he put back in his mouth and yells to the players to line up for their pre-practice stretches.

Mac watches for a few minutes and then realizes he really does need to go.

After all, today's practice is noncontact, but tomorrow's won't be.

That means Mac has twenty-four hours to figure out how to keep Ryan off the field while also keeping his job.

CHAPTER 4

By the time Mac gets home, he realizes he can't figure out what to do on his own. He needs some advice. And anytime he needs sports advice, he knows who to turn to.

Samira Ahmad, sports expert.

Samira knows every fact and stat there is to know about seemingly every sport. If you've got a question about sports, Samira can probably answer it.

The question Mac wants to ask is simple enough: "How do I report an off-the-record conversation without reporting it?"

Okay, maybe that's not really a sports question. It involves an athlete, but it probably doesn't require knowledge of sports history.

Then again, Samira isn't only a sports guru. She's also Mac's best friend. If he's going to talk with *anyone* about his dilemma, it's going to be his best friend. Which brings up another question: *Should* he be talking with anyone about Ryan's concussion? Does "off the record" mean he can't share the information, even privately, with anyone?

It's a fair question, but one that occurs to Mac too late. He's already FaceTimed Samira and told her everything.

"Is he nuts?" Samira says. "Hasn't he ever heard of Ken Stabler? Frank Gifford? Lou Creekmur?"

Mac isn't sure even he has heard of Lou Creekmur, and outside of Samira, he's probably the biggest sports fan in school.

"They're all football players, right?" he says.

He's in his bedroom, at his desk, wondering if he should be Googling Lou Creekmur and how to spell it.

Samira nods through the screen. "They're all football players who suffered from CTE."

"Brain damage?"

She nods again. "It stands for Chronic Traumatic Encephalopathy."

"That's why I'm calling you," Mac says. "It's crazy, right? But how do I stop him from playing?"

"Have you told him about Greg Feasel?"

"Another player with CTE?" Mac asks.

"Along with playing football, he went to med school," Samira says. "But by the end of his life, he was having trouble having conversations with other people. His injury had turned him into a completely different person."

It was definitely a powerful story, but . . .

"I don't think Ryan's going to change his mind because of some player he's never heard of," Mac says.

Samira looks puzzled. Is she surprised that Greg Feasel's story wouldn't persuade someone to take a game or two off? Or is she surprised that some people don't know who Greg Feasel is? Probably both.

"What about other people?" Samira says.

"What about them?"

"What if you told other people about Greg Feasel, or Paul Oliver, or . . ."

Samira keeps listing names, but Mac tunes her out—not because she's making a bad point, but because she's making a good one. She's right. Maybe he can't report on Ryan's head injury, but there's nothing to stop him from writing about other players who suffered concussions. He doesn't know whether Ryan reads his sports blog, but it's a pretty good bet that he does. Most athletes at Canyon Middle do.

". . . or Kevin Turner," Samira says, still listing names of players, "or Joe O'Malley, or Junior Seau, or . . ."

"Sorry to interrupt, Samira," Mac says. "But I have a blog post to write."

THE MAC REPORT
SPECIAL REPORT: CONCUSSIONS

The year was 1993, and the Minnesota Vikings were in the playoffs. Their quarterback was Jim McMahon. He was known for his toughness—for getting back up no matter how hard he'd been hit.

This toughness was on full display against the New York Giants. At one point during the game, McMahon got crunched by not one but *two* Giants.

Years later, he learned the hit had broken his neck.

At the time, what he knew was that he couldn't feel his legs. Luckily, the loss of feeling didn't last long, and he was able to shuffle to the sidelines. But he didn't stay off the field for long. This was the playoffs, and McMahon was determined to keep playing.

It didn't take long for McMahon to get hit again—this time on the head. Once more, his legs went numb.

Looking back, McMahon regrets his decision to return to the field—not just in that 1993 playoff game but throughout his time in the NFL. He had somewhere between three and five diagnosed concussions. He has no idea how many hits to the head went undiagnosed.

However many it was, they took their toll on him.

He now suffers from dementia and often has trouble remembering close friends' names. Sometimes he'll leave the house and forget how to get home again.

McMahon will likely struggle with dementia for the rest of his life. He's understandably upset—with the league for not taking better care of him and with himself for acting, in his words, "like an idiot." Football culture and his own competitiveness told him to play through injury, to stay quiet about it, to get back on the field as fast as possible.

These messages, as much as the hits themselves, have also taken a toll on his life.

Mac doesn't stop there. He researches and writes several more blog posts about players dealing with the consequences of their concussions.

George Visger, a former lineman for the 49ers, brings notebooks with him everywhere he goes. He takes notes on what he's doing. If he doesn't do this, he won't remember what he did the day before.

Merril Hoge, an ex-Pittsburgh Steeler running back, once got hit so hard in the head that he actually stopped breathing for a while. He had to spend over a year relearning how to read.

Al Toon was a wide receiver for the New York Jets. His last concussion, he said, "felt like a cannonball hit me in the back of the head." He was told by doctors that he needed to retire; if he got struck in the head even one more time, they said, he might never recover. He followed their advice.

Mac writes about George Visger and Merril Hoge and Al Toon and others too. By the time he goes to sleep, he's written half a dozen posts.

The only thing left to do is wait and hope that Ryan reads them.

CHAPTER 5

Either Ryan didn't read Mac's blog posts, or he did but still doesn't care about the risk he's taking by playing with a concussion.

If he did care, he wouldn't have arrived to band practice with ear plugs.

Mac watches Ryan take them out of his pocket and put them into his ears.

What am I supposed to do now? Mac wonders.

After all, I've done all I can, haven't I?

If Ryan is this committed to acting stupidly, maybe I should let him.

Part of Mac wishes he hadn't seen Ryan bang his head against the field. Then he wouldn't be faced with this impossible choice.

The ear plugs must be working a little; someone's instrument screeches loudly, and Ryan winces but doesn't nearly collapse to the floor like he did yesterday.

Who am I kidding? Mac asks himself. The second he decided to become a journalist, he signed himself up for impossible choices. He knew exactly what he was getting himself into. He was agreeing to follow stories, wherever they led. It's his job to tell those stories, which is to say it's his job to tell the truth.

And that's what he needs to do now: find a way to tell the truth about what happened at the end of the football game.

Ryan's trying to cover up that story, and Mac can't let him.

"Sorry."

It's Dave Corcoran's voice.

"For what?" Mac asks, turning to him.

Dave uses his trombone to point to Mac's tennis shoe. There, on the toe of the shoe, is a big glob of spit.

"It was an accident," Dave says.

Mac knows this is a lie. He knows it because this isn't the first time Dave has "accidentally" emptied the spit from his instrument onto Mac's shoe. He also knows it because he can see Dave's lips curling into a smile behind his mouthpiece.

Usually, Mac would give Dave a piece of his mind. He's even been known to retaliate with a spit glob of his own.

But today, it isn't worth it. Dave is gross, obnoxious, and jealous, but Mac doesn't have time to retaliate. Even if he did, he tells himself, he should really be more mature than that.

That's when he spots Dave's high school letter jacket draped on his chair. Despite not being in high school or playing in the high school band, Dave brings the letter jacket with him wherever he goes. He claims he plays in the high school jazz band and that's where he got the letter for his jacket. Mac thinks he's probably lying—either about playing in the high school jazz band or about earning the letter. But frankly, Mac's never cared enough about Dave or band to fact-check Dave's story.

As Mr. Paulsen lifts his arms to start a new song, Mac yanks Dave's jacket off his chair and uses a sleeve to wipe the spit off Mac's shoe.

Okay, so maybe Mac did have time to retaliate after all.

Dave's eyes open wide in anger. He looks like he wants to yell at Mac, but he doesn't. Dave's way too serious about band to interrupt the middle of a song.

Mac gets back to thinking about Ryan's concussion and what he's going to do about it.

"Ready?" Samira asks.

Mac looks at Annie Chin. She was recently hired as

Coyote Canyon Middle School's athletic trainer. That's where he, Samira, and Annie are—in the athletic training room. Behind Mac is a treatment table; behind Annie is an ice machine. A few moments ago, Annie took a poster off the wall that has a cartoon brain on it and a list of concussion symptoms. It was Samira's idea for Annie to hold up the poster. It was Mac's idea to interview her and put the interview up on his blog.

Annie nods her head that she's ready.

"Go ahead, Samira," Mac says.

Samira has agreed to film the interview with her phone. When it's done, she's going to spend the rest of their lunch period putting in closed captions, in case kids try to watch the video on mute during class. That's the point of the poster too—they're trying to get the concussion symptoms information out there as quickly as possible. Maybe if they can start a school-wide discussion about concussions, Ryan will feel pressured to change his mind about playing with one. Of course, Annie doesn't know the particulars of their plan. She just knows she's new here, and two kids have asked to help her introduce herself and a serious health issue to the Coyote Canyon student body.

Admittedly, Mac and Samira's real plan is a bit of a long

shot. But there are only a few hours left before football practice starts, so anything is worth a try.

Samira points at Mac and Annie to let them know she's started recording.

"Hi, fellow Predators. I'm here with Annie Chin, our school's athletic trainer. She's agreed to—"

He doesn't get to finish his introduction because Coach Jorgenson opens the door.

"Oh, sorry to interrupt," he says. "Just looking for a few rolls of tape . . ."

His voice trails off as he backs out of the room. Before

he closes the door behind him, though, he squints. He appears to be reading the poster that Annie's holding.

After the door shuts, Samira says, "Should we start from the top?"

Mac nods and is waiting for Samira to point at him when the door opens again.

And again it's Coach Jorgenson.

"Can I speak with you, McKenzie?" he asks.

It's technically a question, but it doesn't sound like it.

"In my office," Coach says.

He doesn't wait for a yes or no.

Samira pockets her phone. Mac wheels out the door.

Annie Chin lowers the poster to the ground as she watches Mac leave.

Mac isn't too sure himself, but he knows it's pretty rare for Coach Jorgenson to issue orders, even ones that are technically questions.

"Coach?" Mac asks.

"Close the door, would you, McKenzie?"

Once again, it isn't a question.

"What's going on?" Mac asks, stopping in front of Coach's desk.

"I was going to ask you the same question."

"Coach?" Mac asks again.

"I read your articles. The ones you wrote last night," Coach says.

Mac opens his mouth to say something, but he decides to let Coach keep talking.

"Must've been six, seven articles about professional football players who got their bells rung."

"They got concussions, Coach," Mac replies.

"Isn't that what I just said?"

"You said they had their bells rung. That's a euphemism."

"A euphemism?" Coach asks.

"A way of making light of a serious topic. Concussions are a serious topic, Coach."

"Whoa. Ease up, McKenzie," Coach raises his hands in mock surrender. "I wasn't trying to make light of anything. Why do you think I called you in here?"

"I don't know," Mac says, which is true.

Coach looks at Mac for a beat. "So you can tell me who on my team has a concussion," he says.

There's a long silence. The two of them stare at each other for what feels like minutes. Mac keeps expecting Coach to say something else, but instead, he just adjusts the flat brim of his baseball cap and keeps waiting for Mac to say something.

"Look, Coach . . ." Mac says, but he can't think of anything else to say.

"Yesterday at practice, you mentioned somebody else speaking to you off the record. Then you wrote about all those players. Today, I find you interviewing Ms. Chin about concussions." Coach shook his head. "Tell me I'm wrong. Tell me you're not trying to send a message that one of my players had his bell—er, excuse me—was concussed."

Mac may not be able to tell Coach the specifics of an off-the-record conversation, but that doesn't mean he has to lie about it. Silence, as far as he can tell, is his best option.

"That's what I thought," Coach says. "If you can't tell me I'm wrong, then I'd appreciate a name, McKenzie."

"I . . . can't, Coach." Mac looks apologetic. "That information was given to me off the record."

Coach stares at him some more. Finally, he says, "Tell you what, McKenzie. Stop by practice today, okay? I think you'll find that I take concussions pretty seriously."

As opens the door and Mac backs out of the office, Coach says, "Oh, and Mac?"

"Yeah, Coach?"

"Feel free to consider everything that happens to be on the record."

CHAPTER 6

It looks colder outside than it is. Maybe it's the gray sky or the wind. Like yesterday, Mac is sitting at the edge of the parking lot, slightly above the practice field, and he's surprised he's not shivering.

It feels like he should be doing *something* other than just sitting there, waiting for Coach Jorgenson to arrive and do . . . whatever it is he's going to do.

Unlike yesterday, the players are wearing their helmets and pads. Some are throwing footballs back and forth, others are casually stretching. They have no idea what's about to happen either. The difference is that they *think* they do. They assume practice is going to be pretty much like every other practice.

There's a loud whistle, made louder by the fact that Mac is so close to it.

A second later, Coach walks by, heading toward the fence separating the parking lot from the field. He opens the gate, steps through, and tells everyone to gather around and take a knee.

"Gentlemen," he says, "it's come to my attention that

one of you was seriously hurt in our game a couple nights ago. For whatever reason, you haven't come clean about this injury. It would be one thing if the injury were to a limb—a leg, an arm. Don't get me wrong, failing to fess up about a messed-up limb would be misguided. The sooner we know about it, the sooner we can start rehabbing it. There's also always the chance that by continuing to play on it, you'll do permanent damage."

Coach looks at each of his players.

"Frankly," he continues, "I would understand if there are players among us who haven't reported a dinged-up elbow or a tweaked ankle. I don't condone it, but I understand where you're coming from. Football is a violent game; to play it, you have to endure all manner of nicks and bruises and pain. Sometimes, the best way to do that is to try to forget the pain, pretend it's not there. But I'm not talking about an injured limb; I'm talking about an injured brain."

Coach points to his hat. Like yesterday, it's covered by a stocking cap and a baseball hat.

"Opting to play through an injured brain isn't just misguided, gentlemen. It's plain stupid. And dangerous. You're not just risking your future football career; you're risking your future, period. Yes, football asks you to be tough, but it shouldn't ask you to be stupid. That's why I'm asking you to come forward. Maybe we can't change football culture everywhere, but we can change it on this team, here and now."

Mac's eyes are locked on Ryan, wondering whether he'll heed Coach Jorgenson's request.

The answer is no, he won't.

It's not just that Ryan doesn't stand up; the kid doesn't even flinch.

"I was afraid of that," Coach says. "In that case, I have no choice but to cancel practice. If need be, I'll cancel tomorrow's too. And the next day's. And then I'll cancel our game against Forrest View."

The players have been silent throughout Coach's speech, but they're grumbling now.

"That's not fair," more than one player says.

"It's not our fault," says someone else.

"This isn't about fairness or fault, gentlemen," Coach says. "It's about protecting one another. It's not my job to guarantee your safety. Obviously, I can't do that. But it is my job—it's all of our jobs—to look out for one another. We will not take another snap until we've gotten this player the medical attention he needs. If you'd rather not come forward in front of the whole team, I understand. I'll cancel practice for today and hope to hear from you soon. But I can't in good conscience—"

"It's me, Coach."

Everyone turns their head to Ryan. He's still on one knee.

From where Mac's sitting, he can hardly hear Ryan. Unlike Coach Jorgenson, Ryan isn't projecting his voice.

Mac's not sure if that's because he's embarrassed or nervous or something else.

Coach nods, tells his assistant coach to get the team started, and walks toward Ryan.

While the rest of the players do team stretches, Coach talks to Ryan, who is still on one knee. Mac can't hear what they're saying over the team warm-up.

Eventually, Ryan gets up off his knee and shuffles off the field. He takes off his helmet, dejected.

It's not until he's at the fence that he notices Mac.

"I didn't tell him," Mac says.

Which is true, technically speaking.

"You told everybody," Ryan says.

Which is also true, in a way.

Mac now realizes why Ryan was so hard to hear. He might indeed be embarrassed or nervous, but he's also furious. Seething. It's taking him considerable effort to keep his voice in check. If he wasn't speaking so quietly, he'd be screaming.

"If we lose to Forrest View," Ryan says through gritted teeth, "it's your fault."

PREDATORS NAME NEW QB
by Mac McKenzie

It took two full practices, but Coach Jorgenson has named his starting quarterback for tomorrow's game against Forrest View.

Ever since a few days ago, when Ryan Mitchell acknowledged having concussion-like symptoms, Coyote Canyon Middle has been auditioning quarterbacks to take his place.

Aidan Karl, the Predators' strong safety, had trouble holding onto the snap.

Dylan Seracki, their tight end, showcased a good arm and good size, but was too slow getting rid of the ball.

Running back Carter Sanchez looked pretty good under center, but not as good as he looks from the backfield. Against a rival like Forrest View, they're going to need his rushing yards.

The last player to take a few snaps was wide receiver Ethan Young. There wasn't anything in particular about Young that made him stand out. At maybe five-and-a-half feet tall on his tiptoes, he's rather short for a quarterback. In fact, he literally got on his tiptoes to see over the line. Speaking of his feet: Young's aren't particularly nimble. Still, he did show an ability to move around in the pocket to buy a little time before throwing. His arm is average at best but appears to be fairly accurate. He has a quick release.

"Plus, he knows all the plays," Coach Jorgenson said with a laugh. "That's pretty important."

Of course, knowing the plays is one thing; executing them is another.

Young's main job will likely be to take care of the football and not make any costly mistakes.

Against an excellent Forrest View squad, that might be easier said than done.

It also might not be enough.

CHAPTER 7

As Mac sits on the sidelines in the moments before the game, he wonders if his last article was too harsh. He'd listed weaknesses for each player who bravely volunteered to play quarterback until Ryan got back on the field. Sure, analysis was sometimes part of his job. And yeah, he was mostly echoing what Coach Jorgenson had told him during his latest interview. But these players weren't *just* players; they were classmates and friends.

He looked to his right and his left. On either side of him were Predator football players.

He wouldn't blame them if they were more than a little angry at him. Along with criticizing the skills of their teammates, he had masterminded a way to get their starting quarterback off the field. Obviously, that's not how *he* saw it—he was just trying to do what he felt was right—but he wondered if it's how *they* saw it.

It's definitely how Ryan Mitchell viewed the situation. For the first time all season, Ryan had showed up to school today—game day—without formal attire.

"No suit and tie?" Mac had asked.

Frankly, Mac knew how disappointed Ryan was and just wanted to lighten the mood by changing the subject. "What's the point?" Ryan had replied, practically spitting the words out. "Coach won't let me even stand on the sidelines during the game. He says my only job is to rest and recover."

Now here Mac is, on the same sideline Ryan's been banished from, surrounded by Ryan's teammates, some of whom he analyzed harshly in an article for all to see.

His harshest words had been for Ethan, whom he'd basically called short, slow, weak-armed—mediocre at best.

Mac watches Ethan jog onto the field and make his way to the huddle—the huddle that he's now in charge of.

Mac looks once more to the players standing next to him. They haven't said a word to him, and he's been assuming they're giving him the cold shoulder. But he now realizes there's another possibility. Maybe they're just nervous. After all, they're not talking to each other either. Their eyes are fixed on the field.

The huddle breaks, and the Predators get lined up. Forrest View is already there waiting for them. They dig into the turf with their cleats.

Ethan doesn't get under center right away. Instead, he surveys the defense.

Everyone in the stadium must be asking the same question: Is Ethan up to this task?

We'll find out soon enough, Mac thinks.

Forrest View clearly doesn't think so. Coach's plan is to run it down Forrest View's throats all night, and they know it. Their linebackers and strong safety creep up to the line of scrimmage to close any holes in the defense. After getting the handoff, Carter Sanchez, the Predators' running back, will have to slam into a wall of bodies.

That's when Ethan does a surprising thing. He audibles. Rather than simply calling, "Hut!," he changes the play.

When he finally takes the snap, he fakes the handoff, looks up the field, and floats a pass to a slanting wide receiver. The ball doesn't have the zip on it that Ryan's passes do. Instead of a tight spiral, it wobbles a bit, even flutters. But it lands perfectly and gently into the receiver's hands.

Forrest View has put almost everyone on the line of scrimmage. There's no one left in the secondary. The Predators' wide receiver has one guy to beat, and then he's streaking toward the end zone.

Touchdown.

Just like that, it's Coyote Canyon 6, Forrest View 0.

The Predator fans erupt. So does the Predator sideline. Everyone jumps up and down and cheers and bangs each other's shoulder pads.

Maybe everything will be okay, Mac thinks.

For one thing, it looks as though he and Coach Jorgenson may have underestimated Ethan Young.

For another, the players on the sideline are clapping Mac's shoulders too.

COYOTE CANYON BEATS RIVAL WITH BALANCED ATTACK

by Mac McKenzie

With Coyote Canyon (4−0) missing their starting quarterback, Forrest View (3−1) seemed to have one goal in mind: stop the Predators' stellar running attack. They routinely had seven and even eight players in the box.

It worked. At the half, running back Carter Sanchez had a grand total of negative three yards.

But stopping the run didn't stop the Predators' offense. Backup quarterback Ethan Young took advantage of the openings Forrest View's overeagerness created. He lobbed screen passes over their outstretched arms. He hit crisscrossing receivers over the middle and in stride. Often, the receiver caught the ball with a full head of steam and room to run.

In the first half alone, Young completed nine passes in a row.

By the time Forrest View backed off the line of scrimmage, it was too late. The Predators had built a three-touchdown lead and were happy to resume handing the ball off. Sanchez finished the game with a well-earned 67 yards.

"The first time the

new kid changed the play, I wasn't pleased," Coach Jorgenson admitted. "But the play he changed to was a 78-yard touchdown. It's hard to stay mad at that."

The Predators' 35–7 victory puts them alone atop the conference standings.

CHAPTER 8

That weekend, Mac's basketball team has its first captain's practice of the season.

Mac is one of the team's two captains.

His team's still a good month away from officially starting the season, and most of the players who show up are rusty. It's been a year since some of them have dribbled or shot a basketball.

He and the other captain, his buddy Ty Warren, decide to have a scrimmage. They divide the players into two teams. At first, the basketball is predictably ugly. Lots of missed shots and basketballs ricocheting off wheels and out of bounds.

Mac does his best to refrain from shooting. The best way to knock off rust, he knows, is to knock down shots. Nothing gives a player more confidence than a few made baskets. For this reason, Mac spends the scrimmage finding open teammates and encouraging them to let it fly.

On the one hand, he's being a good, selfless teammate. On the other, it's easy to be selfless when he (and everyone else) knows he'll end up getting his fair share of shots.

During a water break, Mac and Ty decide that the first team to score 40 wins.

"Maybe we should make it 50," Mac says. "These guys could use the extra practice."

"You think I don't know what you're doing?" Ty says, laughing. "You're trying to give yourself more time to mount a comeback."

It's true that Mac's team is losing—35 to 29.

"What are you talking about?" Mac says, smiling.

"You know exactly what I'm talking about," Ty responds. "You're about to take over the game—at least that's what you think. I think you're good, but you aren't *that* good. We only need a couple more buckets, and there's nothing you can do to stop us."

Mac thinks about this, then smiles again. "Challenge accepted," he says.

Right off the bat, he drains a three. "35–32," he says as he hustles back to play some defense.

Back on the other end of the court, he waits for the ball to swing to the corner, then pounces. Ty's teammate Sam is trapped. If this were a real game, Sam might call a timeout, but it's a scrimmage, so he doesn't have that option. He attempts to pass through Mac's outstretched

hands but fails. The ball glances off Mac's wrist and is picked up by one of Mac's teammates.

While everyone else converges on the loose ball, Mac pivots on his chair and races down the side of the court. "Hey!" he yells.

His teammate finds him and throws a baseball pass Mac's way.

Catching the ball, Mac lines up another three.

SPLASH!

"Tie ball game," he says.

"I didn't know you knew how to count by threes," Ty replies.

Ty brings the ball up the court. Mac decides to trap him right as he crosses half court, but Ty anticipates the move. He zips a pass to the guy Mac is supposed to be defending, then powers his way past the two chairs trapping him and calls for the ball for an easy give-and-go.

"37–35," Ty says.

It's Mac's turn to bring the ball up the court. When he does, he sees that Ty isn't the only one ready to stop him at all costs. Ty's team is barely even guarding anyone else; instead, they're bunched together, watching Mac closely.

The idea is to make anyone other than Mac take the shot. Mac passes to one of his teammates, then follows his pass to set a screen. Or that's where it looks like he's headed. Instead, he cuts toward the basket and raises his hand. His teammate finds him, and Mac makes an easy layup.

"Don't say it," Ty says.

Mac says it anyway, grinning. "37–37. Looks like we're all knotted up again."

Mac switches onto Ty and then immediately sags back into the lane. He's baiting Ty to take a three, and Ty knows it. But he shoots anyway.

"You're not the only sharpshooter around here," Ty says.

This is false. Ty is an excellent point guard, but a sharpshooter he's not.

The ball thuds against the rim and, after a nice outlet pass, ends up once again in Mac's hands.

Mac approaches the three-point line.

"We all know you're going to make it," Ty says, "so make it quick, would you?"

Mac releases the ball. He's the only one who sees it go in. The others are already shaking hands and saying, "Good game."

CHAPTER 9

Mac gets to the band room early on Monday. He needs to put oil on his trombone, but doing this is always risky. For one thing, it is almost impossible not to spill the oil, and once it gets on your hands, it takes hours for it to come off.

Oiling the slide became even trickier when Dave Corcoran was around. He inevitably "accidentally" bumped Mac's hand with his trombone.

Mac takes his time throughout the whole oil-applying process. He uses the sleeve of his shirt to carefully remove the almost-full bottle of oil from his trombone case and equally carefully sets it down next to him. Then he lifts the various parts of his trombone out of the case and slides them together.

He's pulls the cuff of his shirt over his hand again and reaches for the bottle of oil.

It's not there.

He's just about to turn around when a hand grabs his shirt collar and pulls it back.

The next thing he feels is the slimy oil gushing down his neck and back.

The now-empty bottle of oil clatters on the plastic seat next to him.

"Are you kidding me, Dave?!" Mac yells.

Spit on the shoe is disgusting enough—but emptying a whole bottle of oil down his shirt? That's borderline evil.

Mac whips around and sees that Dave's not the culprit.

Ryan is.

"Good news," Ryan sneers. "I passed the concussion protocol over the weekend."

Mac is covered in oil that's still trickling down his back, and he's confused. Why the sarcasm in Ryan's voice?

"Isn't that good news?" he asks.

"It's irrelevant news," Ryan says. "Coach just called me into his office and told me he was going to start Ethan anyway."

With that, Ryan turns and walks out of the band room.

"Makes sense," Samira says, taking a bite of a french fry. They're in the cafeteria.

"What does?" Mac says. "Pouring oil down my back?"

He's reaching behind him, under his shirt, using a napkin to wipe off the drying oil. When the napkin is soaked, he rips his paper lunch bag in half and uses that instead.

"Coach choosing Ethan over Ryan," Samira says.

"How does that make sense? Ryan's been their quarterback all year. He's one of the leaders of the team."

Samira eats another fry. "Ethan is much more efficient from the pocket," she says. "I ran the numbers."

"Of course you did," Mac says. He should have known that she would have.

"It's not just that he completed more passes," Samira continues, ignoring Mac's jab. "It's the kind of passes he attempted. Most of them were between five and fifteen yards. Ryan doesn't throw many of those because he likes to go for the big play. When he does throw them, he's not as accurate."

Samira's school bag is on the chair next to her. She unzips it and takes out a notebook.

Mac watches her leaf through the notebook. Based on all the numbers in there, you'd think it was her math notebook, but Mac knows better. This notebook is devoted to sports analysis. So are probably two or three more in her backpack.

Samira finds the page she's looking for.

"Check out this head-to-head comparison in yards after catch," Samira says, handing Mac the notebook.

Mac does. As usual, Samira has done her homework.

He tries out a few more arguments on Ryan's behalf.

"Ryan is undefeated," he says.

"So is Ethan," Samira counters.

"Ryan's a leader."

"Ethan led them down the field all night."

"Ryan has a better arm," Mac says.

"That doesn't make him a better passer." It's clear Samira isn't going to budge on this one.

"Fine. You win," Mac says.

He takes the other half of the paper bag and continues sopping up the oil. Mac is still furious at Ryan for pouring that oil down his back. But he isn't feeling sorry for himself, at least not really. He's actually feeling sorry for someone else . . .

Mac shakes his head. He needs to snap out of it. The person he's feeling sorry for is Ryan—the guy who did this to him.

THE MAC REPORT
SPECIAL REPORT: BACK, BETTER THAN EVER

In my last blog entry, I wrote about NFL players whose careers and lives never recovered after devastating concussions. That got me thinking. What about the opposite situation? What about players—quarterbacks specifically—who get injured but come back better than ever?

One of the best examples I can think of is Peyton Manning. By 2011, Manning had spent over a decade as one of the best QBs in the league. He'd won four MVP awards and gone to two Super Bowls, winning one of them.

Along the way, Peyton pinched a nerve in his neck. The injury required surgery that sidelined him for the entire 2011 season. When he first woke up from the surgery, he tried to sit up in bed, but his right arm—his *throwing arm*—couldn't support his weight. Months later, after another neck surgery, Manning found himself unable to throw more than five yards. Some believed his arm would never fully recover.

His team, the Indianapolis Colts, was concerned enough that it decided to move on without Manning.

They had their sights on Andrew Luck, the highest-rated quarterback coming out of college since . . . Peyton Manning.

Manning refused to believe he was finished. He joined the Denver Broncos and had one of the greatest comebacks in sports history. While with the Broncos, he set the all-time record for touchdowns in a single season (55), won his fifth MVP award, and took home another Super Bowl trophy.

My second example of a player returning from injury is Manning's greatest rival, New England Patriots QB Tom Brady. On the first game of the 2008 season, Brady took a step with his left foot, heaved a pass, and was hit below the knee by an opposing player. The injury looked nasty because it was. He tore both his ACL and MCL. Like Manning, it would take him an entire season to recover.

But when he finally did make it back onto the field, he picked up right where he'd left off. That season, he won his second MVP award. He's won a total of five Super Bowls, two of them since coming back from injury.

In other words, it is not only possible to come back from injury, but it's also possible to have *success* after coming back from an injury.

CHAPTER 10

Ryan is back in uniform for the Predators' next game. But he doesn't look happy about it.

Mac knows he's on bad terms with Ryan, but he can't help asking, "What's with the clipboard?"

"I'm like a second coach," Ryan says.

He doesn't say it with any enthusiasm.

"Really?" Mac asks.

"That's what Coach says," Ryan answers, clearly not believing it himself. "I'm supposed to write down anything that seems important—Middlefield's defensive tendencies and alignments, possible play selection, anything I can think of that might be helpful to Ethan. During timeouts or other stoppages of play, Coach wants me to share my words of wisdom. He says my insights are really important to Ethan and the rest of the team."

"You don't believe him?" Mac asks.

"Look at the scoreboard."

Mac does. There's four minutes and change left in the first quarter, and the Predators are already up two

touchdowns. "Does it look to you like Ethan needs my 'really important' insights?"

Mac turns to watch the game. Ethan is under center, examining the field. Ethan decides to back up into a shotgun formation. This is a new wrinkle to the offense that Coach added this week in practice. It was Ethan's idea. For the last few days, the center has practiced snapping the ball through the air to Ethan.

Ethan calls, "Hut!" The football doesn't have a lot of juice on it, but it gets to him. As soon as it does, Ethan pivots and throws to a receiver at the line of scrimmage.

The cornerback is playing a good seven yards back, which is exactly how many yards the play goes for—seven. It's second and three, and rather than huddling up, Ethan calls for the team to line up again. This is another thing Ethan asked to add to the offense, and it appears to be working. Middlefield is scrambling to get lined up themselves. It's still the first quarter, and they look gassed.

Ethan hands the ball to Carter, who scampers his way for a six-yard gain and another first down.

Mac turns to Ryan. He wants to tell Ryan that this could be a worthwhile experience; he might really learn something from watching Ethan. But Mac doesn't know how to say this without making it sound like an underhanded compliment. It'd be like calling a plumber and asking if he wanted to watch another plumber work on your sink. True, the plumber who's just watching might really learn something—but who wants to learn something from a direct competitor?

To his surprise, Ryan is scribbling away at his clipboard.

"Can I ask what you're writing?" Mac says.

Ryan tilts the clipboard. It says: "This never would have happened if it weren't for you. Go ruin someone else's life."

Mac sighs and finds a different spot on the sidelines to watch the game.

QB, OFFENSE SHARP AGAIN
by Mac McKenzie

For the second game in a row, Coyote Canyon Middle's offense was a model of efficiency. The Predators (5–0) made it look easy against a Middlefield (1–4) team that had no answers for quarterback Ethan Young's quick-pass approach.

Middlefield has struggled on offense all season, but on defense they've found ways to get to the quarterback. They entered tonight's game with the most sacks in the conference. Try as they might, though, they were unable to put Young on his back. Not only did they fail to record a sack; they never laid a finger on the Predators' QB.

"When your quarterback is getting rid of the ball like that," Coach Jorgenson said, "it makes it almost impossible for the defense to put any pressure on him."

Young marshalled the offense down the field for drives of 86, 72, and 91 yards.

The final score was lopsided—42–14—but not lopsided enough. Middlefield's points came late in the fourth quarter, when the game was already decided and the starters were off the field.

CHAPTER 11

"Aren't you going to give me my change?" Mac asks.

It's early in the morning, and as usual, he's in the gym, shooting. The only difference is that Ty Warren, the co-captain of his basketball team, has decided to join him.

"Nope," Ty says. "My court, my rules."

He pushes his wheelchair with his right arm while dribbling with his left.

"How is this your court?" Mac asks. "You don't even go to school here."

It's true. Ty and Mac are on the same *district* team, but Ty goes to school in the next town over.

"My dad's a construction worker," Ty says.

"So?"

"So he built this school with his bare hands. He put together this court, board by board."

Mac's pretty sure this is nonsense. Wasn't the school—and the court along with it—built in the 1950s? Ty's dad wouldn't have even been born yet. But Mac doesn't have time to object, because Ty's already talking again. This is a recurring problem: Ty is almost always talking. Luckily,

Ty's good at talking, so come to think of it, it isn't much of a problem at all.

"Change," he says.

Mac tracks down the rebound and says, "What are you talking about? You just missed."

"Exactly. I need more practice."

"That's not how this works," Mac says.

"It is on my court," Ty says. "The other way doesn't make any sense. If someone makes a shot, they clearly don't need the extra practice as much as someone who misses. It's simple logic."

Ty is still holding his hands out for the basketball. Mac has to hand it to him; Ty has a point. Mac passes him the ball.

Ty shoots and misses. "Change," he says again.

"How many tries do you get?" Mac asks.

"Until I make it," Ty says, as though it's obvious.

"I could be sitting here all day," Mac says.

"Welcome to the club. You know how many times I've had to sit there and pass you the ball because you never seem to miss? No wonder I can't make anything. I've spent most of my career rebounding your swishes. When you finally miss one, I'll take one shot, miss it, and then it's your

turn all over again. You're lucky I'm such an all-around great guy," Ty says, grinning. "If I weren't, I might resent you."

He shoots. The ball rattles around the rim and then falls out. Ty hold up his hands for the ball again.

"Ryan Mitchell resents me enough as it is," Mac says. He passes Ty the ball. "I don't need you resenting me too."

"Ryan Mitchell?" Ty asks.

Maybe it's the fact that Ty goes to a different school, but unlike Samira, he's usually oblivious to any drama away from the court.

"Forget about it," Mac says.

"Can't forget what I don't know," he says happily. He launches another shot. This one goes in. "Change," he says.

"What about your court rules?" Mac says.

"Come to think of it," Ty says, "the regular rules are better. I mean, why reward failure? That only encourages more failure. It's success that should be rewarded."

"How do I know you're not going to change the rule again?" Mac asks.

"All objections to the recently changed court rules should be submitted in writing to the head of the rules committee," Ty says.

"Who's the head of the rules committee?" Mac asks, even though he already knows the answer.

"Me," Ty says. Then takes another shot.

CHAPTER 12

In band, they're playing the same compilation of movie theme songs they played the day Ryan collapsed to the floor.

For trombone players, that means a lot of whole notes and long rests.

Instead of counting during these rests, Mac looks over to the percussion section. Ryan's there, banging away at a snare drum.

You're welcome, Mac thinks. *If I hadn't gotten you the rest you needed, you might still be collapsing every time you hear a loud noise.*

Mac doesn't mean to be petty or bitter. He *still* can't help but feel sorry for Ryan. His whole life was playing quarterback for the Predators, and now that's been taken away from him. It must be devastating. But does he have to be such a jerk about it?

The truth is that Mac always liked and admired Ryan. And honestly, he never expected Ryan to give up so easily. He wants to tell Ryan that he had a tough break, that everyone does, and that the way to respond to it isn't to take his bad luck out on others.

Out of the corner of his eye, Mac sees Mr. Paulsen gesturing with his right arm to the trombone section. In a few seconds, it will be time to play again.

He lifts his trombone to his mouth and his eyes to his music stand. He inhales and exhales a note, then stretches the slide. So does Dave Corcoran, except instead of stretching the slide below or to the side of Mac's music stand, he "accidentally" tips Mac's stand over.

It crashes loudly against the chair in front of Mac and then rattles on the floor.

People stop playing to see what happened.

By now, Dave is playing innocently with his slide under his own music stand.

And Mac is so angry so quickly, it's overwhelming.

"*What is the matter with you?*" he yells at Dave. "Huh? Quit grinning behind your mouthpiece, and explain to me why you're always acting like a jerk!"

Mac is vaguely aware that *everyone* has now stopped playing, but he drowns out this awareness by yelling even louder. "I'm sorry, okay? I'm sorry you care more than I do, but I'm still first chair! I'm sorry that you put in more time practicing, but our teacher decided I was better than

you! Here's an idea: Instead of constantly tormenting me and being a jerk about everything, why not channel that frustration into getting even better? Ever thought of that? Why not just get better and better, and beat me fair and square?"

Honestly, Mac has no idea where this outburst came from. Yes, Dave Corcoran is an insufferable jerk—but he's known that for a long time. This isn't even the first time Dave has knocked over Mac's music stand.

Nor does Mac realize that he spent most of his tirade looking right at Ryan instead of Dave.

What he *does* realize, now that his blood has stopped

boiling and is currently draining from his face, is that the whole band is staring at him. And that Dave looks positively horrified.

He can't think of anything else to do or say other than, "Sorry."

Apparently, Mr. Paulsen doesn't know what to do either, because he just clears his throat, raises his conductor's wand, and says, "Where were we?"

Apparently, Mr. Paulsen is too focused on next week's concert to deal with Mac and Dave.

A few minutes later, everyone's back to playing the Indiana Jones theme song.

Mac bends over and picks up his music stand. As he sets the music book on the stand, he happens to notice that Ryan's not playing either.

As always, Mac is leaving school late. He's just submitted his recap of the girls' tennis match and is pushing his way through the school door and into the parking lot. The first person he spots is his mother, waiting for him in the otherwise empty lot.

The second person he spots is Ryan.

He's sitting on the curb. Practice must have ended

an hour ago, but Ryan's still wearing his football gear. He tosses and catches a football absentmindedly before noticing Mac.

"Nice speech today," Ryan says.

"Speech?" Mac asks.

"To Dave." Ryan stops tossing the ball and looks up at Mac.

"Oh. Right," Mac says. "Guess I didn't think of that as a speech so much as a meltdown."

"You were pretty intense," Ryan agrees. "You okay?"

"Sure," Mac says. "How about you?"

"Off the record?"

Ryan's got a wry smile on his face, so Mac risks a smile as well. "At this point that goes without saying, right?"

Ryan's smile doesn't fade, so Mac hazards another joke: "Just don't tell me you're actually a cyborg who's planning to take over the world for humanity's own good, because I definitely can't keep that secret."

Ryan shakes his head. "If I were a cyborg, I'd never tell you. Not after losing my starting spot to a measly human. It'd bring shame to my cyborg pod."

"Pod?" Mac asks.

"That's what we call our family units," Ryan says matter-of-factly.

"Makes sense." They don't say anything for a bit. "Same question as before," Mac says. "You okay?"

Ryan answers with another question: "How much time you got?"

Mac looks at his mom in the car and opens and closes his hands twice. It's his way of signaling he needs twenty minutes. Last year, they both realized that his job as a reporter sometimes required him to stay late interviewing people or finishing articles. The hand signals are one of several methods they devised to communicate with one another. The rule is simple enough: He gets to have one time extension, no more than twenty minutes in length. After that, he's getting in the car and going home, regardless of whether he's finished with his interview or story.

Mac's mom starts up the car and leaves the parking lot. This all happens so subtly that Ryan doesn't even notice.

"I'm all ears," Mac says.

Ryan takes a breath. "I guess I should start by saying I'm sorry. For putting you on the spot. For blaming you when I got beat out for the starting spot."

"And for pouring oil down my back," Mac adds.

Ryan laughs. "Yeah—that too."

"Apology accepted."

"The truth is, I think I was ashamed by how scared I was," Ryan says.

Mac is surprised. "Scared? Of losing your starting spot?"

"Probably. But it was more than that. I think what I was most scared of was what these last couple weeks taught me."

Mac waits for Ryan to continue talking.

"I always thought of myself as a great teammate," Ryan says. "I didn't care about stats—just wins. I'd sacrifice my body if it meant getting one more first down. I'd put the team on my shoulders and lead them down the field for a game-winning touchdown."

"All that stuff is true," Mac says.

"Right. But it's also all about me. It turns out I'm only a good teammate if I get to be the star. We've gotten two huge wins in a row, and I've somehow managed to hate every second of it."

Mac laughs, which surprises Ryan.

"I tell you I'm selfish, and you laugh?" Ryan says. "Aren't you supposed to be a good listener? Isn't that, like, your job?"

"Sorry . . . It's just, *everyone* is selfish like that." Mac says. "Or at least everyone who's any good. Great players don't just want to win; they want to win *themselves*. I'm not saying we should be proud of it—but being ashamed isn't right either. I mean, do you think Robert Parish cared as much about the NBA championship he won as a benchwarmer for the Bulls as he did the ones he won as a star for the Celtics?"

"Robert who?" Ryan asks.

Sometimes Mac forgets that not everyone knows as much about sports as he and Samira—not even other athletes.

"Sorry," Mac says. "He was a basketball player."

"That reminds me," Ryan says. "There's a rumor going around that you play basketball."

Mac nods.

"And that you're good. I mean, *really* good."

Mac tilts his head, considering the compliment, and nods again.

"So what would you do if someone joined the team who was better?"

Mac shrugs. "In the end, I hope I'd find a way to make it work."

Ryan shakes his head. "How about before the end?"

"I'd work that much harder in the gym, I guess," Mac says. "I'd get as good as I could possibly get. I wouldn't concede my role on the team until I absolutely had to for the good of the team."

Mac pauses, then adds with a small laugh, "But yeah, I think I'd have a hard time not holding it against the guy who was taking over my spot."

Ryan laughs too, then asks, "Do you think I'm as good as I can get?"

"No. But there's only one way to find out." Mac looks at the empty parking lot. "It's the intermediate passes you've got to get better at. Do you want to try?"

"Try what?" Ryan asks, confused.

Mac is moving away from Ryan, talking over his shoulder. "Throwing some of the intermediate routes." He lines up along an imaginary line of scrimmage. "Let's start with button hooks."

It takes Ryan a second, but then he catches on. Standing up, he takes a few strides and crouches under an imaginary center. "Hut!" he yells.

He shuffles backward as Mac jolts forward for 10 yards, then spins his chair on a dime. Ryan steps in and throws a perfect spiral . . . that sails way over Mac's head.

Mac swerves around and tracks down the football. He tosses it back to Ryan.

"You know what was wrong with that pass?" Mac asks.

"That it was way too high?" Ryan says.

"That, and the fact that you didn't start throwing it

until I'd already turned around. This is a timing route, man. You've got to get rid of the ball quicker."

Mac lines up on the imaginary line of scrimmage again. "Ready whenever you are," he says.

He does another button hook. And another. And another.

After five minutes he changes up the route. First to outs, then ins, then slants, then crosses.

Mac's arms are beaded with sweat despite the cooling weather by the time his mom pulls back into the lot.

"I have to go," he tells Ryan. "But we can do the same thing every day of this week if you want to."

All Ryan can think to say is, "Thanks."

"Need a ride home?"

Ryan shakes his head. "I only live a few blocks away."

Mac says, "See you tomorrow."

THE MAC REPORT
SPECIAL REPORT: COMEBACK SUCCESS

For some reason, I can't seem to get quarterbacks and injuries off my mind these days. Today's blog post focuses on NFL stories of one QB getting replaced by another and *both* quarterbacks having success.

I mentioned Peyton Manning last time, and he's one of them. Not only did he go on to have great success in Denver, but the Colts' Andrew Luck also had great success, with several solid seasons of play.

The Green Bay Packers moved on from Brett Favre after the 2007 season, and his replacement, Aaron Rodgers, is one of the best quarterbacks in the league. As for Brett Favre, he had maybe the best season of his career in 2009 with the Minnesota Vikings.

Many considered Joe Montana the best quarterback of all time when he went down with an injury in the early 1990s. While he was recovering, his backup—Steve Young—stepped in and became a star in his own right. The 49ers ultimately decided to part ways with Montana, and it was the right choice: Young had become an elite-level QB. But Montana was by no means finished. He went to Kansas City and had a couple of excellent seasons. He even made the Pro Bowl in 1993.

And thus concludes my Special Report posts about football players coming back from injuries . . . I hope. I guess I just think it's important for players coming back from injury to know that it's not only possible, but also possible that the injured player *and* their replacement can have success.

CHAPTER 13

All week, Ryan has been practicing with Mac in the parking lot. With each completed pass, he seems to have gained confidence.

But now here they are, minutes from the start of the Predators' game against West Clover, and his shoulders are slumped.

"Chin up, Mitchell," Mac says. "Do you know about Steve Young and Joe—"

"Montana. Yeah, I know."

"How about Brett Favre and—"

"Aaron Rodgers," Ryan interrupts.

"Ha! So you *have* been reading my blog posts."

Ryan looks up from his clipboard. "No offense, but they don't really help. There's nothing I can do to get back into the starting lineup."

He's talking under his breath so only Mac can hear him. He doesn't want to make a scene. It's the first truly cold day of fall. As Ryan speaks, Mac can see the breath come out of Ryan's mouth.

"What do you mean?" Mac asks.

"This isn't the NFL. No matter how much I improve, there's no reason that Coach will ever know it. Ethan gets almost all the snaps during practice. Most of my reps are with you, in an empty parking lot. That means we're the only two who know whether I'm getting any better."

"You just have to wait for your chance," Mac says. "Do your best to stay optimistic."

"That's the thing," Ryan mutters. "Brett Favre and Joe Montana had other teams they could play for. But unless my family moves, my only option is the Predators. That means my chance will only come for pessimistic reasons. Either Ethan gets injured or he starts to play really bad. What kind of a teammate hopes either of those things happens?" Ryan shrugs his shoulders and continues. "Like I said. It's just the way things are. No one had any idea Ethan could play quarterback until I went down. He was just a not-that-fast receiver who nobody really paid attention to. Not even Coach. And now I'm the one Coach has likely forgotten about."

"Mitchell!" Coach hollers, almost right on cue. "What is wrong with you?"

Mac and Ryan watch Coach storm over. His face is red, and not only because it's cold.

"Coach?" Ryan says.

"You heard me," Coach Jorgenson says. "Where are your sleeves?"

Ryan looks down at his bare arms. They're covered in goose bumps.

"Was your plan to stand there and freeze to death?" Coach says. "What if we need you? How are you going to play quarterback if you're frozen to death?"

"Sorry, Coach."

"Don't be sorry," Coach says. "Be smart."

Then he takes off the bulky winter jacket he's wearing and drapes it over Ryan's shoulders.

Ryan tries to say thank you, but Coach has already stormed off in the other direction.

"Maybe he hasn't totally forgotten about you," Mac says.

PREDATORS WIN AGAIN, BUT JUST BARELY

by Mac McKenzie

In a gridiron battle between an undefeated team and a winless one, the result was predictable. Coyote Canyon Middle (6–0) left West Clover's (0–6) field with another victory.

But it wasn't easy.

On an unusually cold day, the Predators' offense appeared at times frozen in place.

At first, it looked like the game was going to be a blowout. Quarterback Ethan Young opened the game with a 79-yard drive. Young connected with wide receiver Matt Ojekwe on a pretty back-shoulder route for the game's first touchdown.

It ended up being the game's only offensive touchdown.

Coyote Canyon added to their lead late in the game when strong safety Grant Fowler swiped a pass out of the air on his way to the opposite end zone.

The score was still 14–0 when the final buzzer sounded.

"A win is a win," Coach Jorgenson said.

The Predators remain in first place as they gear up for a rematch against long-time rival Forrest View.

CHAPTER 14

"What happened?" Samira asks.

"You literally just read my game recap," Mac says.

They're at lunch, but Samira is apparently too perplexed to eat. Her tray is still full of food. She squints at Mac's game recap on her phone and tilts her head, as if by doing these things, the words on the screen will give her more information than she currently has.

"Where's the box score?" she asks.

This is an absurd question. "You're the one who does the box scores, not me."

In fact, she's the one who provides most of the stats he uses in his game recaps.

"I told you," Samira says, "I couldn't get a ride to the game."

They sit there in silence as Samira continues to squint at her phone. "It doesn't make any sense. Why would Ethan have a bad game against the worst team in the conference? Did he stop throwing five- to fifteen-yard passes?"

Mac shakes his head. "He just didn't complete very many of them."

"So . . . what? He all of a sudden became a less accurate thrower?"

"Actually, he had to throw the ball away quite a bit."

"Why didn't you say that before?" Samira says, finally peeling her eyes away from the phone. She asks the question as though learning that Ethan had intentionally thrown the ball where no one could catch it changes everything.

"Does it change the fact that he had a bad game?" Mac says.

"No," Samira says. "But it changes *why* he had a bad game."

"Why did he have a bad game?" Mac asks.

Samira stares at Mac and then blinks. "Because no one was open. That's why quarterbacks have to throw the ball away."

"So why wasn't anyone open?" Mac is still unsure what Samira is getting at.

Samira gives one shake of her head and looks at her phone again, as if Mac's article will provide an answer.

"Samira, I wrote that, remember?" Mac isn't sure why he has to remind her of this. "Why would my article know something I don't?"

"Sometimes you're smarter in print than in real life," she says.

Mac's pretty sure she means this as a compliment.

CHAPTER 15

Mac finishes his shooting early the next morning. He's on his way to his locker when he hears sounds coming from the band room.

Musical sounds.

Trombone sounds.

He opens the door and peers inside.

There Dave Corcoran is, in an otherwise empty band room . . . sitting where Mac usually sits. He's literally scooted his chair farther to the left so he can use Mac's music stand.

"You're unbelievable," Mac says.

He must say it loudly, because Dave not only hears him, but jolts around.

"What is this?" Mac demands, rolling further into the room. He reads the sheet of music on the music stand—*his* music stand. "That's what I thought. It's my concert solo. How did you even get it?"

Dave opens his mouth to answer, but Mac doesn't let him. He's got more questions to ask; he's on a roll.

"Did you go through my locker? Do you know how

creepy that is? It's illegal—you realize that?" Mac's not actually sure it is illegal to go through someone's locker, but it probably is, and he's too angry to stop now.

Dave tries to say something again, but Mac isn't finished.

"You get that this makes you a criminal?" he asks. "Is it really worth breaking the law just to play a few minutes of music? Honestly, what is—"

"I didn't steal it!" Dave interrupts. "Ever heard of Google? Go look in your locker if you don't believe me!"

The righteousness of Dave's response catches Mac off guard. "What are you even doing? Why are you here, practicing my solo?"

"I'm trying to do what you said, okay? You said I should get better than you and beat you fair and square. Ever since, I've been coming here every morning and trying to do that."

Mac is skeptical, but Dave definitely *looks* sincere. That stupid smirk he usually wears is nowhere to be found.

"It's still weird that you moved your chair," Mac says.

Dave doesn't dispute this.

CHAPTER 16

If anyone thinks the Coyote Canyon Predators are going to beat the Forrest View 35–7 again, they're quickly proven wrong.

Forrest View returns the opening kickoff for a touchdown.

After Coyote Canyon goes three and out, the Flash run a double reverse that nets them 52 yards. Two plays later, their quarterback scrambles away from the Predators' rush and finds his tight end wide open 30 yards downfield. A quarterback draw and an extra point makes the score 14–0 with eight minutes left to go in the first quarter.

Fortunately for Coyote Canyon Middle, the defense figures things out. They don't give up any points for the next three quarters. At the beginning of the fourth quarter, the Flash quarterback botches a hand off with his running back. The ball bounces on the field and in and out of a few players' arms before being scooped up by the Predators' linebacker, who runs 26 yards into the end zone.

With eight minutes to go in the fourth quarter, Forrest

View decides to bleed the clock. They run the ball three straight times, then punt it back to the Predators.

With just over three minutes left on the clock, Coyote Canyon starts their next drive at their own 24-yard line. After a brief huddle, they line up. Ethan crouches under center, his head on a swivel. He stands up to get a better look at the defense, then crouches again.

Mac, sitting in his usual sideline spot near the bench, waits for him to call, "Hut!"

But he doesn't do that. Instead, he stands up again.

Ethan turns to the sideline, then back to the field, then back to sideline.

He raises his arms and touches the fingertips of one hand to the palm of the other.

The referees whistle for a timeout.

Shaking his helmet, Ethan jogs to the sideline. Mac assumes he's going to talk with Coach Jorgenson, but he's mistaken.

Ethan's not looking for Coach. He's looking for Ryan.

"You need to go in for me," Ethan says.

Ryan looks confused. "Are you okay?"

"I'm fine," Ethan says. "But you need to go in for me."

"You all right?" It's Coach Jorgenson. He's just arrived.

"I'm fine," Ethan repeats. "But Ryan—"

"Needs to go in for you," Coach says. "I heard you before. What I'm trying to ascertain is why. Are you injured?"

Ethan shakes his head. "I'm fine," he says for a third time.

"Well then what's the matter with you?" Coach asks. "What's going on?"

"The only thing that's the matter with me is that I don't have a very good arm," Ethan says.

The referee blows his whistle to indicate the timeout is over. Ethan raises his hands again and signals for another timeout.

The Predator fans aren't happy about it.

"What in blazes are you doing, Young?" Coach says. "You're wasting all our timeouts!"

"Look." Ethan takes the clipboard out of Ryan's hand and opens his own hand for Ryan's pen. Ryan gives it to him. "Here's how the defense is lining up against us." He draws a bunch of X's and O's. "West Clover did the same thing. They're only rushing three guys. Everyone else is lining up between five and fifteen yards back. It makes it almost impossible for me to complete intermediate passes. I can't beat this defensive strategy."

Ethan looks up at Ryan and points at him with the pen. "At least not as effectively as you can. With your arm strength, you can sit back in the pocket and wait for receivers to stretch the defense and get open downfield. It's our team's best option."

The referee blows his whistle again.

This time it's Coach Jorgenson who calls for time.

Boos come raining down from the stands.

"He's right," Coach says. "Mitchell—grab a football and take a few warm-up throws."

"Yes, sir," Ryan says.

As for Mac, he's speechless and dumbfounded. He's never seen anything like this.

As far as Mac's concerned, Ethan Young might very well be the greatest teammate in the history of sports.

PREDATORS COME BACK FROM EARLY DEFICIT

by Mac McKenzie

Coyote Canyon Middle (7–0) found themselves down a touchdown with time ticking away in the fourth quarter. An unexpected quarterback change jumpstarted the offense and led to an impressive come-from-behind victory.

Down 14–7 to their archrival Forrest View, things looked bleak for a team that had scored only one offensive touchdown in the past seven quarters. That's when quarterback Ethan Young called a timeout. Two more timeouts were called in quick succession.

When the Predators finally took the field again, Ryan Mitchell was their quarterback.

He made the most of his opportunity. Mitchell threw three straight completions, all of them significant: 31 yards, 25 yards, and 33 yards. That last throw brought the Predators to the three-yard line. Carter Sanchez broke one tackle behind the line of scrimmage and then dove successfully for the end zone.

Coyote Canyon opted to go for two.

When asked why he didn't just kick the extra

point and go into overtime, Coach Jorgenson dead-panned, "Seemed like it would be quicker to win without an overtime."

Luckily, the decision worked. Mitchell rolled to his right and found all of his receivers defended. The only player Forrest View wasn't guarding was Mitchell himself. He jogged into the end zone to give the Predators a 15–14 victory.

CHAPTER 17

"I've never seen anything like it, Samira," Mac says, his face glowing.

It's late at night, after the Forrest View game. Mac is getting a ride home from his mom.

He and Samira are FaceTiming.

"I looked it up," Samira says. "I'm pretty sure three consecutive timeouts is an all-time record."

"No, not that," Mac says. "I'm talking about Ethan giving up his starting quarterback position. Who does that?"

Samira seems less impressed. "It was the logical thing to do."

"*Still.*"

"It won't work as well next week, unless Ryan is able to make the shorter throws too," Samira continues. "The defense will eventually adjust. They always do."

As always, everything Samira is saying is true. And at any other time, he'd love to hear all of her stats and analysis.

"Let's talk more about it at lunch," he tells her.

She says okay, and they hang up.

Right now, rather than stats and analysis, what he wants

to do is think about what he just witnessed. Ethan Young gave up his spot—*voluntarily*. Mac can't get over it. Sure, it was logical. Yes, it was for the good of the team. But no one knew that until Ethan explained it.

"You seem deep in thought," Mac's mom says.

Mac just nods.

Ethan Young willingly gave up a spot that he had earned, and Mac is trying to decide if he's willing to do the same thing.

"Dave," Mac says.

But Dave doesn't hear him; he's too busy tuning his trombone.

"Dave," Mac tries again.

Dave blasts a single note, almost exactly at the same time Mac says his name. Then he moves the tuning slide slightly in. He blares another note and decides to move the tuning slide back where he originally had it.

He's doing all this while sitting on a chair on the auditorium stage. Tonight, several hours from now, is the fall concert. A handful of students volunteered to set up the stage. Mac is one of them. He asked Dave to help as well, which Dave didn't like. Dave said he'd rather spend the class period practicing his trombone. But Mac told Dave he had something important to talk to him about, so Dave finally agreed to tag along.

Unlike all the other students setting up the stage, Dave only grabbed one chair and one stand: his own. Then he plopped down on the chair and began this painstaking tuning process.

"*Dave!*" Mac says for a third time.

Finally, he's gotten Dave's attention.

"What?" Dave says, annoyed. "Now I'm going to have to start the whole process over."

"Listen to me," Mac says. "The truth is that I think you're irritating and obnoxious and not a very good person." Mac's tempted to stop there. Dave's currently doing lip exercises, and Mac can see his spittle shooting into the air. "But I also know how much playing trombone means to you, and my guess is that you know my solo tonight better than I do." Dave literally starts playing the solo right then and there. Mac has to push the trombone away from Dave's lips to get his attention again. "What I'm trying to say is that I've decided you can have my solo."

For a brief second, Dave looks shocked in a good way. Then he asks, "What's the catch?"

"There's no catch," Mac assures him.

"This isn't a trap?"

Mac shakes his head. "Nope."

"You're just going to hand over the solo?" Dave asks.

"I think you're the right guy to play it."

"Thanks." Dave sounds genuinely grateful. "Actually, I've been thinking of ways to make the song better. Like, what if—"

Mac holds up his hand. "That's between you and Mr. Paulsen," he says.

He backs away to get more stands.

"You coming to my concert tonight?" Mac asks Samira at lunch.

"I would," Samira says, "but there are sports on TV tonight." She isn't looking at Mac.

"There are always sports on TV," Mac retorts.

Samira turns to Mac. "Exactly," she says.

They both laugh.

"Suit yourself," Mac says. "Concert night means chocolate malts and strawberry pie."

Samira thinks about that. "After careful consideration, I've decided to skip the concert but join you for chocolate malts and strawberry pie."

Mac looks at Samira and thinks she might just be his hero.

CHAPTER 18

Mac's feeling pretty good about himself.

The band has finished the first two pieces, and Mr. Paulsen turns to the audience to introduce the soloists. In a few minutes, Dave will be the center of attention on stage, living out his dream, and it will all be thanks to Mac.

Mac sees now that his need to be first chair was mostly out of spite and was downright petty. Why did he ever want a solo in the first place? By giving the solo away, Mac can sit back, relax, and daydream about chocolate malts without any whipped cream and strawberry pie with real strawberries and none of that syrup from a can.

"Without further ado," Mr. Paulsen says, "please give a hand for our trombone soloist."

The audience claps.

And claps.

And finally stops clapping.

It's only then that Mac snaps out of his daydream and realizes two things.

First, the entire band appears to be looking at him.

Second, Dave is still sitting next to him.

Under his breath, Mac asks, "Dave, what are you doing?"

"I . . . I can't do it," Dave says, also under his breath.

"What are you talking about?" Mac can't believe this is happening.

Dave looks as if he's frozen to his seat. "My body . . . It won't move," he says. "I'm too nervous."

So much for Mac making dreams come true. He reaches across to Dave's music stand, takes the sheet of music—he'd left his own copy of the solo in his locker—and lifts his trombone.

The audience politely claps, probably relieved that the awkward silence is over.

Mr. Paulsen looks relieved too.

Mac takes a deep breath and begins to play.

After the concert, Mr. Paulsen asks to see Mac in his office.

"What happened out there, McKenzie?" he asks.

Mac shrugs. "Dave froze. I'm sure he just needs a little more experience with this sort of thing."

"What does Dave have to do with anything?" Mr. Paulsen looks genuinely confused.

It was only then that Mac discovered Dave had neglected to mention to Mr. Paulsen that he was going to take the solo instead. In fairness to Dave, Mac had forgotten to mention the switch too.

Mr. Paulsen is obviously less than pleased.

After Mac apologizes for the third time to Mr. Paulsen for the mix-up, he finally leaves his office. The office is attached to the band room, and it's a good thing it is, because the lights in the band room are off. If it wasn't for the light coming out of Mr. Paulsen's window, it would be too dark for Mac to see where he's going.

As it is, he can barely make out the chairs and music stands and . . . person?

"Hello?" Mac says.

The person doesn't answer. But they're sitting in Dave Corcoran's chair, and they're about the same size and height as Dave Corcoran, so . . .

"Dave? Is that you?"

"How'd you do that?" the voice says.

It's definitely Dave's voice. Mac would recognize that whiny voice with his eyes closed.

"Do what?" Mac asks, moving closer.

"Stand up there and play the solo in front of all those people," Dave says. "You were a little flat, and you rushed the third section; I mean, I'm not saying you played it perfectly . . ."

Mac wants to say something sarcastic: "Thanks for the feedback, jerk." Or, "I'll keep that in mind next time I bail you out." But he knows Dave well enough that he's pretty sure Dave doesn't realize he's being a jerk.

"But you did it," Dave continues. "You played with all those people watching. You obviously hadn't practiced enough"—again, Mac wants to say something snarky but restrains himself—"but you got up there anyway. I stayed up all night getting the song perfect. I could play it with my eyes closed. Seriously. I'll show you. The lights are off, so even if I cheat, I still won't be able to see the notes."

Mac's eyes have adjusted to the dark, and he watches Dave pick up his trombone and bring it to his mouth.

"I believe you," Mac says. "Really. You don't need to prove it to me."

Dave lowers the instrument.

"Is that why you're here?" Mac asks. "Sitting in the dark? To prove to yourself that you can play the solo?"

Dave doesn't say anything, but he nods his head.

That should probably be Mac's cue to leave. If sitting in the band room in the dark helps Dave cope with choking at the concert, then Mac should get out of the way and let him sit here as long as he needs. It's not Mac's job to chaperone one of his classmates. He's got a malt to slurp and a slice of pie to devour.

But he can't just leave—not when Dave is acting like this.

"How do you do it?" Dave asks again. "How do you play in front of hundreds of people?"

Mac thinks about it. "Practice," he says.

"I practice way more than you," Dave says.

Leave it to Dave, Mac thinks. *He's always got to one-up me on everything.*

Mac chooses to ignore this slight. "Yeah, but you don't practice in front of a crowd."

Dave turns his head. "You do? How?"

"Every time I play basketball."

"Oh." Dave's clearly not impressed.

"I don't just play basketball," Mac says. "I play it really well."

Mac's never said that out loud before. It's not his personality to brag. But he's pretty sure Dave won't take it that way. As far as he can tell, Dave appreciates facts, and Mac's guessing he doesn't mind when others brag if they're simply stating facts.

"When you're really good at basketball," Mac says, "you

end up with the ball in your hands a lot. Everyone expects you to make big plays—to take and make game-winning shots. If you miss, you let everyone down—the crowd, your teammates, even yourself."

Mac has Dave's attention again. "So, how do you make sure you don't miss?"

"You don't," Mac says. "Sometimes, you're going to miss. But guess what happens then?"

Dave waits for him to answer his own question.

"Nothing," Mac says. "I mean, people are upset. You're upset with yourself. But pretty soon, everyone more or less moves on. And here's the thing, Dave: If you're good enough, you'll get lots of other chances to get it right. And when you do get it right, you get to be the hero . . . right up until you screw up again."

"So I'm supposed to practice in front of other people? Isn't that weird?" Dave asks.

Mac thinks about reminding Dave that he's sitting on his own in a darkened band room to prove to himself that he can play a song without looking at the notes. That's pretty weird too.

"When I shoot on my own, sometimes I imagine there's a crowd watching me," Mac says. "There's only ten seconds left on the clock. Then nine . . . then eight. If I make the shot, we win the game; if I miss, we lose. Maybe you could do the same thing when you practice? Imagine you're playing a solo at a concert?"

"I could try that," Dave says.

He actually sounds pretty excited about it. Mac doesn't have the heart to tell him that imagining a crowd might help a little, but it probably won't be enough. The only way to get over the fear of failure is to actually, genuinely fail and then pick yourself up and try again.

That's something that Mac's pretty sure a person has to learn on their own.

In any case, it's not something he's going to explain right now—his parents are waiting for him.

"I have to go," he says. "If you want to take the next solo, it's yours. Just make sure you tell Mr. Paulsen first, okay?

By the time Mac gets to the lobby and he heads to the parking lot with his parents, almost all the cars have left.

His phone dings in his pocket.

A text message from Samira. She's already at Baker's Batch. "Malt? Pie? Where r u?"

"Mom. Dad." Mac says, looking at his phone. "Go on ahead. I'll be there in a sec." Mac starts to type a response.

His mother sighs. "Make it quick, Stewart."

"Hey, Mac."

It's Ryan. He's standing in his concert clothes—white dress shirt, dark pants—and he's holding a football.

"Hey. Look, I have to go," Mac says, pressing "send" on his message to Samira and putting his phone in his pocket.

At least that's what he would have said, if Ryan had let him get the sentence out.

"Coach gave me the nod to start next week," Ryan says.

"Cool. Listen—" Mac tries to say. He knows his parents have been patient enough already.

"I really don't mean to bother you, but I was thinking, if my midrange passing game isn't sharp next week, Holy Mary's defense will adjust and find ways to prevent the longer throws."

"You were thinking this?" Mac asks. The analysis sounds oddly familiar.

"Well, you know your friend Samira? I ran into her today at school. Really, it was more like she ran into me. But she made some really good points."

"She always does," Mac agreed.

"I really don't mean to bother you, Mac, but—"

"You already said that."

"Yeah. Sorry. Any chance we could throw some routes? I figure the parking lot is well enough lit that you'll be able to see the ball okay."

Mac sighs. He looks up at his parents' car. He opens and closes his hands twice.

The car starts up and pulls out of the lot.

"You've got twenty minutes," Mac says.

Twenty minutes later he gets in his parents' car, and they tell him that Baker's Batch isn't in the cards tonight. His baby sister is at home with a babysitter, and they've already made the sitter wait longer than planned.

Mac checks his phone. It seems Samira has given up on him too. She was kind enough to send him two pictures: one of a chocolate malt, no whipped cream; the other of a slice of strawberry pie.

CHAPTER 19

As it turns out, changing quarterbacks changes everything else too.

Against Holy Mary Middle, Coyote Canyon doesn't just play better through the air; they also play better on the ground. With Holy Mary's secondary backing up to defend for the big pass play, running back Carter Sanchez often finds himself with room to operate. When Holy Mary adjusts by sending their linebackers to plug holes on the defensive line, Ryan fakes the hand off and dissects the defense with shorter throws.

At some point in the third quarter, a timeout is called.

It isn't a player on the field who calls it.

Nor is it Coach Jorgenson.

It's Ethan.

Mac isn't sure a player is even allowed to call timeout from the sidelines. But the refs let him do it.

Mac looks for Coach Jorgenson to see if he minds having one of his players call timeout. If he does, he doesn't show it. In fact, he looks interested.

Ethan waves Ryan over.

Ethan points to the clipboard he's holding and says, "We should start doing double moves."

"Double moves?" Ryan asks.

Ethan nods his head. "It's the next logical step."

He sounds just like Samira, Mac thinks. Who knew there was another Samira walking the Earth?

By now, all the skill players are surrounding Ethan's clipboard. He attempts to explain what he means but then reconsiders. "Tell you what. I'll do one," he says. "I'm going to take your place for this series, Paul," he tells one of Coyote Canyon's wide receivers.

Paul doesn't object.

Maybe it's because the Predators are winning comfortably, but Coach doesn't object to Ethan inserting himself into the game either.

Then again, maybe it's because Coach has never seen a player like Ethan before. After his willingness to give up his starting quarterback spot, no one on the team can doubt his motives. Lots of players say they just want what's best for the team, but Ethan seems to actually mean it.

The ref blows his whistle, and the offense, minus Paul and plus Ethan, jogs onto the field.

Ryan takes the snap while Ethan runs a standard out route.

Or that's what it looks like, until Ethan turns and takes off upfield.

Ryan fakes the out, and the Holy Mary cornerback bites. He lunges in front of Ethan, hoping to pick off Ryan's pass and run for the opposite end zone.

By the time the cornerback realizes his mistake, Ethan is running free up the sideline.

Ryan launches the ball deep and with plenty of arc.

The football falls into Ethan's hands, and he runs the rest of the way to the end zone.

PREDATORS PUT ON SHOW

by Mac McKenzie

The last few games have been touch and go for the Predators (8–0). Tonight's game was purely *go*. Their offense was on the move throughout, and Holy Mary (4–4) was helpless to slow them down.

Perhaps the highlight of the game was a long touchdown pass from Ryan Mitchell to Ethan Young, who only two weeks ago was the team's starting quarterback.

The offense appears to be firing on all cylinders. Just don't tell Young that.

"There are lots of things that we can add," Young said. "Little things, big things, tweaks here and there."

Coach Jorgenson said, "Thirteen years old, and this kid already sounds like a coach. He's got the art of saying everything and nothing at the same time down pat."

Ryan Mitchell was standing nearby. "I have no idea what you're talking about," he told Young, "but I look forward to having you explain it to me."

Right now, it's the rest of the conference that needs to learn how to stop Mitchell. According to the team's unofficial statistician, Mitchell completed 24 of 31 passes today for 287 yards and three touchdowns.

"Really? Is this for real?" Mac says to the Predators' unofficial statistician.

They're at lunch.

Samira has just reached into her backpack and brought out a mini cooler.

"Why did you think I sent you the pictures?" she asks.

"I thought you were rubbing it in that you got to have them when I didn't."

"Is that what people do?" Samira says. "You need to get some new friends."

"That's what I was thinking. But then you go and do something like this."

Samira lifts the lid of the cooler. She takes out a Tupperware and a thermos.

"One chocolate malt, no whipped cream. One slice of strawberry pie," she says.

She's even brought a fork for him.

"You're the best," Mac says. "One question, though: The band concert was two nights ago. Why didn't you bring the malt and the pie to lunch yesterday?"

"Okay, so maybe this isn't the exact same malt and pie I took a picture of," Samira admits.

Mac laughs. "That's what I thought."

"I mean, that's really why I texted you the pictures—I swear. I was totally planning to bring them to you yesterday. But there was a game on at the restaurant, and it went into overtime, and I got hungry, so . . . By the time the game ended, I sort of forgot about your malt and pie."

"You mean you forgot about me," Mac says. They both know he's just giving her a hard time.

"But then you were so mopey yesterday at lunch," Samira says, "I figured I better go get you your stupid food so you'd stop talking about it and start talking about sports again."

Mac would keep giving her a hard time, but he has a malt and a slice of pie to eat.

A few minutes later, his mouth full of food, he says, "You totally forgot about me."

"The game went into *overtime*," Samira reminds him.

"Good point," he says, washing the pie down with a sip of chocolate malt.

If there's one thing they can both agree on, it's that sports pretty much always comes first.

"That reminds me," he says, looking at the clock on his phone. "I have to go. Coach Miller agreed to talk to me about the upcoming basketball season."

Mac thanks Samira for the food and heads off for his next interview.

ABOUT THE AUTHOR

Paul Hoblin lives and teaches in St. Paul, Minnesota. He's written several other sports books, including *Foul*, which *Booklist* called "unbearably tense," and *Archenemy*, which won ALA's Rainbow Award.

ABOUT THE ILLUSTRATOR

Simon Rumble lives in the United Kingdom. He has worked as an illustrator in the creative industry, world-wide, for over twenty years.